# V E I N E N

# VEINEN

a short novel by

## JEAN COQT

the third part of
**Skagen a novel of Europe**

translated from the french by

## charles lunaire

*for cathérine*

*Healdsburg : Ear Press : 2015*

# Contents

# 1. Break in the forest

THE ACTUAL BORDER-CROSSING (he said) into Luxembourg was unnoticeable, and he negotiated it by simply crossing the road next to the memorial park, following it for a while, then leaving it in favor of leaf-strewn forest paths.

Luxembourg — the country — is in fact criss-crossed with footpaths. You could make a month's tour of them, after inventing a strategy for sleepovers. Of course in the right season you could simply make do with a blanket and maybe a tent. You need fairly stout shoes, because the country is rumpled. Here, for example, steep banks rise from the river — the Our — up toward the central forested highland, and the footpath is narrow, often steep, sometimes forced to rely on rude steep staircases, some of them quite long.

Just as often, though, there's a break in the forest. A sudden pasture, or a view down toward the river, with perhaps one of those strange duck-blinds — that must be what they are — perched on stilts, mounted on wheels so they can be moved from one location to another, with a long ladder to get up into the cabin. They look like toys; they look like sculptures.   They look like things Philip Guston might one day paint.

Another time the path will lie just outside the forest on the uphill side, past a lush green pasture stretching further up the hill to the right, the west, with a row of neatly spaced, evenly sized, carefully pointed wooden posts laid out along the path.   Someone's about to drive them, when he gets time to get the tractor out, and string a wire along; it's time to move the cattle out of their barns onto the spring pasture.   Everyone here uses electric fencing, easily set up and taken down, moved from one location to another, and much less intrusive on the gentle landscape than the three strands of barbed wire we're used to, not to mention the woven field-fencing.

That, however, is well in the future.   In these times there's no money for such things; and even if there were money the fencing itself is simply not to be found, not for love nor ready money.   All loose metal was rounded up long ago for the war.   And anyway there's no need to fence the cows, there are plenty of kids to mind them, follow them from one pasture to another, and follow them back home at the end of the day.   There hasn't been a wolf seen in nearly a lifetime.

He thinks of such things, walking through Tintesmillen, or is it Tintesmühle — have to get used to various spellings, as German gives way to Luxembourgish.   Tintesmillen: dye-mill, he thinks, there is much to verify later, when reference material may be at hand, and it's time to prepare a report. Now he need only lodge a few things in mind, fastening them to a little song to sing silently to himself.   The rhythmic ease of walking, even on difficult terrain, and the fuzzy context of not-quite-understood close-set languages, seduces the mind, makes it content to adjust, to get along.

Not that there isn't science and history at unexpected moments. At Tintesmillen, for example, he knows, a considerable amount of research and fieldwork had been going on. Frequently water samples were taken, requiring elaborate though small and careful small ditches and traps — think of the *acequias* among the orange trees in Seville — to look into the health of the local *moules perlières*, those delicious little pearl mussels, so common, so numerous in these Ardennes, whose numbers had lately been declining, who knows why — perhaps another casualty of the war.

The war is no longer close; he's left it behind in Belgium; the sound of the guns carries into this forest, but muffled, muffled like memory. He turns his collar up against the back of his neck with some difficulty as the straps of his knapsack press against it. Enough food for a couple of days, and plenty of water at hand, and no one shooting at me or for that matter at anyone else either. He doesn't want to stop, though, it'll be better to leave Belgium as far behind as possible, Belgium and the territory it had seized and the guns that had persuaded the peasants.

He wants to stop, he is tired, but he didn't want to stop here, and his mind raced ahead of his feet, part of it singing its silent song full of observations and memories, another part numb from yesterday's noise and fear, a third part, his favorite part, contemplating the things it knew, a few dates, a few things people had told him were facts, a number of stories, and the stray remembered things, the taste of carbonnade, the smell of gunpowder and horse, the sound of uncle's bagpipe, the touch of a woman, the sight of the square box bed in the corner and the fireplace at the end of the room and the doorway and the cat and the hens. The sound of the hens, a drowsy sound, but this was neither the time nor the place to rest.

A dye-mill could probably be put to good use. Cauldrons, firewood, abundant clean water. A boy or two to chop and carry firewood and mind the water-channels; a woman or two who knew the right plants, herbs and grasses, even certain trees whose bark was needed. Vinegar of course, white vinegar, and clean rags. These were the things a dye-mill would provide, of course. These things and a track, a track wide enough for a donkey and its panniers, but not wide enough for a cart or a wagon. There were enough trees in the flat places, and enough rough outcroppings on the steep hillsides rising above the river, to make a wider road very unlikely. And anyway who would suspect a dye-mill would lie concealed within this thick forest? Is anyone there? Hello? Please answer...

## 2. A bleak opening

STARTLED AT ANOTHER POINT by a slow, repetitive pop-pop-pop off somewhere ahead of us: a slow Diesel engine, perhaps?  Ten or twelve minutes later there it is: a road crew, men in flannel plaid shirts and bright orange overalls driving posts with a portable pile-driver, installing a new guard-rail along the narrow two-lane country road leading toward Dasbourg-Pont, which the footpath has risen to join for a few hundred meters before leading back into the forest.

Dasbourg-Pont, where the guidebook had promised a café. In its time Dasbourg-Pont had been a fairly important customs frontier, the only bridge across the Our for several leagues, on a road winding through valleys among these hills, German on one side stretching east across the forest toward the grain country, west on this side through the forest to the mines.  A bleak opening, now, into what had been a pretty landscape: a busy gas station (Luxembourg still favored for relatively low gas prices) whose remarkably unhelpful clerk, a dark, thick-set woman in her fifties, was surly, even, when asked about the café.  And it closed of course. What's left for us: a bus stop with potentially useful schedule information. And, of course, the bridge itself.

But what about Dasburg, without the "o" and the -Pont? Dasburg, in Germany, is where tonight's hotel was, the only one for miles around we'd found to be open to guests tonight. It's across the Our, at the top of a steep hill, another kilometer along a busy road. We sighed, shouldered our sacks, and hit the road. The Hotel Daytona (!) turns out to be owned by another émigré Dutch couple, from whence I never learned, a pleasant enough couple in their forties I think with an air of resignation, perhaps at the few tourists in this weather. They cater to motorcycle tourists, primarily Dutch — the German motorcyclists prefer to go south to Italy. Perhaps the Dutch do too, and find this a convenient first night's stop on their way.

Dutch names in the guest book: Hilly en Jan, Marc, Miel, Luc, Wim, Tiny. The group from Geldrop, Ridderkerk, Veldhoven, Heereveen, Nuenen, Tilburg, Boxtel, Kerkrade, Eindhoven. *We had a tiptop weekend with you. Delicious sleeping, eating, drinking. We found it really snug, we'll sure be back. The Sambucas went down so good…*

An enormous wooden Harley-Davidson dominates the dining room, and motorcycle parts and accessories, turned into lamps and ashtrays and napkin holders, decorate the tables. A simple beefsteak tonight, with French fries, and one of those too-many-things in-it salads. A little sugary: we're in Germany. We eat hungrily and with pleasure and with a white Moselle wine *en carafe*, very nice; and then a Côtes du Rhone, Cellier des Dauphins, non-vintage. To hell with Sambuca.

In Dasburg we see remains of walls, the professors think they were refuges. Caesar knew about them, they say. He and his troops called them *oppidum*, there were things like that in Rome too; they could only have been permanent settlements. Apartment buildings. Various Germanic and Slavic peoples built similar ramparts, nearly always rings. The Slavs were still building them, far into the middle ages.

They built them of earth, wood and stone, whatever is available. Different folks built them in different ways, depending on what they had, how skillful they were, how much time they had. I suppose they were first built in a hurry, and later, when there was more time, if somebody had enough authority to get it together, they were improved in case there might be further need, or they were allowed to collapse back into ruins, back into the earth, if no one was interested enough to maintain them, or no one had the imagination to foresee future need. So it has always been.

Aage tells me king Gudfred built the Danevirke that way, up in Slesvig, back in 808, to keep vikings in or out, or someone else. Just a dirt wall, like the dikes they built in Friesland, when they dug up peat to burn, and piled spoils in long mounds, and dug drainage ditches. That Danevirke, they didn't abandon it until 1864, in the war with Germany. A thousand years. In that time, how often was it useful, how often was it just something for the sheep to climb? Or a thing of beauty? Or a source of civic pride?

The Dasbourg castle should already be built around 850. One of the oldest castles in the area. Already at the second Norman storm in 892 it was mentioned. King Pepin transferred the area as a foundation of the Abbey of Prüm, it was the Counts of Vianden's fief. The village was at the foot of the fort. First they called it Daysberhc. Later, 1252, was the name Dasberg; 1399 he was called Daisberg. In 1417 Engelbert I, Count of Nassau, inherited it. Dillenburg later, the county of Vianden and we had to call him Lord of Dasbourg. Later, the King of the Netherlands in the House of Nassau. In 1625 there were already thirty-four houses in Dasburg, and the townspeople paid every year a smoked chicken to the Lord, they exercised sixteen days in castle guard duty, and had to make a day of haying for the lord too.

1794: the French Republic liberates the castle and whatever they could find in and around it. 1798: the peasants don't like the idea of being forced into the French army and they revolt. Dasbourg was mentioned several times as a center of the uprising. The peasants lose. 1811: Napoleon I gives the castle and its goods, whatever is left, to marshal Nicolas Charles Oudinot, Duke of Reggio. Reggio is pretty far away, near Naples, a little inconvenient; so the Duke sold it on 13 April 1813 at public auction, under the condition that it be demolished within a year.

Thirty-six investors paid 4400 francs. With the destruction of the archive vault perished also the valuable archive. Four weeks before the arrival of the allies who once were so proud building now become even partially standing remains of the castle ruins except for a few

After the wars of liberation Dasbourg fell to Prussia. At this time, the Our set as a natural border and Dasbourg a border town. Because of steep terrain and poor soil the villagers could barely feed themselves by farming: so most worked as craftsmen, masons, laborers, or woodcutters. Thanks to the flourishing commercial life, the population grew constantly, and the village was usually full of artisans — though the village also owned a brewery.

1900: the emigration began to the industrial cities and to America, and the population was very soon down to 500 souls. Ten of them were killed during the First World War; thirty-one were killed and missing during the Second World War — and eighty percent of the town was destroyed. The Battle of the Bulge, yes?

Dasburg, walls, wooden motorcycle. The weather not too promising this morning, yawn, stretch, Douwe en Egberts. We shoulder the packs, settle the bill, step outside, down the front steps, around the hilltop, down the steep road look

# 3. A vacant spot

I LOOKED OUT THE WINDOW, waiting for the iron to come back to temperature, and saw there two strangers sitting in the shelter across the road, next to the church. I'd never seen them before. I'd never seen anyone at all like them before. What could this mean? Why would two people, a man and a woman, in odd shiny jackets, too colorful, with big knapsacks, why would they come to our village and sit in our shelter next to our church? I gave it up quickly and turned back to my ironing. A lot of work to do that morning.

There they waited a little over an hour for the thrice-daily bus to Vianden, morning, noon, and night. Cold, a little above freezing, but there was a bus shelter with a bench. He read the latest *New Yorker* and stomped about a bit. National road or no, there was no traffic. Next to the bus shelter stood a small church, locked up tight, curiously low, sunken into its plot of land behind a retaining wall, as if the entire country had risen around it by eight feet in the centuries since it had been built.

I never wanted to stay in this miserable so-called restaurant, in this decrepit building that was a hotel a hundred years ago, then a barracks, then a stable, then a house, now a restaurant, and why? No one travels along this road, or hardly anyone, and when they do they don't stop, and when they stop they only complain. Why on earth should I care about them? I have my own work to do, my own miserable life to try to live, and he doesn't make it any easier, I can tell you that. I'll be damned if I open this morning.

The iron has cooled again. That couple is still there in the shelter. And look, now, here comes the old lady out of her house down the road, what will she think of those strangers. She's got her slop-jug as usual, she's going to dump it, as if every right in the world and no one watching, and now look went back inside. If I open my window a crack. Birds sing in the bare branches of the tree behind the shelter, in the green field stretching down to the river. Cold as the mayor's eyes this morning: ironing's not so bad.

The café-restaurant continued to be closed; its proprietor must be away. The old lady stood out in front of her house again and he went down to say hello. She was small and pert, missing a few teeth but beautifully smiling, wearing black stockings, a patterned apron, a dark knit sweater, her thin grey hair close to the skull. She seemed to speak only Lëtzebuergesch, but with gestures and poor Dutch he managed the courtesies, the banalities about the weather, and reassurances that yes, the bus would come, half before one o'clock. They'd lost the whole morning, and had nothing to eat.

Let the iron warm up again. Bother you have to do this so often. Anyway, it can't be helped, who are those strangers, let's step outside have a look at them. An excuse: empty the

trash can.  Oh!  colder than anyone would think this late in
March, they must be cold.  My feet are cold.  Here comes
the old lady, probably wants to know about the strangers, as
if I would know anything about them, or perhaps she
knows something and wants to tell me, warn me perhaps.
Good thing the girl's away in the city at work won't be back
until tomorrow.

Later, say twenty minutes before the bus was to come, the
younger woman whose face he had seen earlier was out in
front of her house.  Well, not really house: her doorway, up
maybe three steps from street level, and the window in
which he had first seen her, to the right of the doorway, pre-
sented a narrow façade at the south end of the long building the café-restaurant occupied; that was probably all she
lived in, three meters by, what, ten or so?  Barefoot, a shawl
draped on her shoulders, dumping something into a dust-
bin, she saw him.

That Flemish girl out on the doorstep.  One day she'll forget the iron and it'll set fire to the place.  Good thing she
almost never goes out, and where would she go?  The bus
to Vianden, shopping for groceries, once a week.  Not twenty minutes there, but then how long in town, and the wait
for the return bus.  Cold, how can she stand to be barefoot
out there.  Hmm, talking to the stranger, who'd knocked on
my door, read the menu, shaken his head.

*Koud is 't, wilt u in voor een kopje thee? spreek je vlaams?*  Oh:
English?  Sorry I speak only Flemish and a little of what
they speak here.  Sit you down there.  Here have I tea, what
kind will you?  Sorry only two or three kind.  That is my
machine, completely new, isn't it?  My man got it for me, to
make some money while he is away.  There will be a bus
twenty after one and take you to Vianden.  Where came

you from? Nederland? So speak you a bit of nederlands, not as Flemish, so difficult to understand up there. Yes?

In a century or nearly two now, how much has changed, how little. He asks her about the old lady who lives down the road. She doesn't know her that well as she can only speak a little of the language here and the old lady speaks no Flemish, naturally, why would she. And yet the king of Nederland ruled this country a hundred years after the separation, or as some of them still call it the revolution. *Verstinn net*, is what she often says, "don't understand." None of them can read or write, of that he's quite certain. Out of the habit.

## 4. Only Flemish

WELL THEN, AS I SAY, beating my way obliquely down the quite steep hill through thick scratchy forest still bare of foliage, down to where I knew a stream must be, cursing the twigs snatching at my cheeks and shoulders and the malevolent roots stubbing my toes or tripping me up entirely, grateful if even a pig track appeared weaving its way through the wretched woods, I spent a couple of hours in near despair.

Then her house, barefoot, putting trash in her rubbish-can, and the old lady hailing her in a surprisingly healthy voice. Clearly they were used to familiar conversations called across the eighty meters or so separating their doorsteps. I couldn't make out a word; their language was completely unfamiliar to me. After a time, though, Younger Woman stepped out her door and addressed me, in Flemish: would I like a cup of coffee, or tea?

Yes indeed, thank you very much, it's rather cold today, isn't it; how can you be standing there without shoes? She smiled and indicated that she was used to it, and indeed her pretty feet seemed completely free from the disfigurements so often caused by years of wearing shoes. I stepped into her kitchen, a small square room whose door opened directly onto the street. A small table, two stools, and an ironing board completely filled the room. The woman seemed to be in her late forties, rather pretty, blonde. The room was warm; she was lightly dressed and barefoot.

No way of knowing when you're safe. Her man could be in the next room, could be the enemy. She could be the enemy. You get used to such situations, my uncle said, and he should know, having survived so many himself in those terrible years, evading the enemy and his own superiors too. His buddies, for that matter, as likely as not to turn him in for a pack of cigarettes. There was a pack on the ironing board. She saw me glance at them. It wasn't yet opened. She handed it to me. I smiled but refused it. You don't begin with debt. She apologized that she spoke only Flemish. She'd come here from Belgium a number of years ago. Flemish, and "a little what they speak here." The ironing board was big and sturdy, and seemed to have a built-in steamer. She seemed to be apologetic.

All that was later, the next day I think. After reaching the stream at the bottom of the hill I slept. The banks were wet from yesterday's rain but I managed. Birdsong woke me: *twaaay, twa twa twa twa tway*, or something like that. Still dark but dawn threatening. I followed the stream always heading south hoping to hear French. Fifteen hours since I'd left, fifteen days or more before any chance of a rest.

Headache from lack of coffee, and hunger beginning in the stomach, and matches spoiled by the rain. Uncle had gone west first, to Flanders, then somehow across — no aircraft

to speak of in that war, hardly any strafing. Occupied territory safer than contested areas the priest told me, and he
knows a lot. How much he must hear in the confessional.
Not just women. The old Spanish road, that brought the
soldiers up from Spain.

Sleep takes care of the fatigue, lying on your back on the
cold stone floor resolves the ache, a cup of tea warms the
fingers and clears the mind, bread and cheese puts stop to
the animal gnawing at your belly, but still you think of
mother in her apron at the door, you'd like to hear a few
words of your own language, a smoke would be nice,
maybe a bit of schnapps. Well the smoke eventually turned
up though schnapps is neither mentioned nor evident. The
old lady next door, no doubt about it. This lonely woman,
no.

Sleep threatens but is out of the question. Not safe; not
appropriate. She already glances at the door. God, I feel
dirty. She reads my mind, tilts the teakettle into a basin,
hands it to me without a word. My cupped hands like small
meat flattened animals lift it to my dry and dirty face, dirty
water runs back into the basin. My eyes thank hers but hers
turn away, not this time toward the door but toward first
the floor, then back over her right shoulder, then finally toward me but with absolutely no expression. There is nothing to hear in this room, not anywhere. In whatever else
there may be of this house, and. There's nothing to be
said. Alone I'd be whistling, maybe she would be humming
some tuneless song, but we are not alone, and there is nothing to say. Goodbye, then, many thanks to you.

## 5. Become quite palatial

IN 1625 THERE WERE already thirty-four houses here in Dasburg, and we townspeople paid every year a smoked chicken to the lord, we exercised sixteen days in castle guard duty, we had to make a day of haying for the lord too. All for protection from the count of Veinen. The peasants may have had it easier, working from dawn to nightfall of course, turning over nearly all they grew.

Suppose, where at other tables, watching curiously, a couple of men, early thirties perhaps, leaned at the bar, a little cheerful. They go out for a stroll, a Martini, ultimately for dinner, and return to the little hotel happy with the choice, the only guests in the hotel, one on the second floor, its windows looking out across to grassy terraces below spruce forest across rooftops on the Rue du Ruisseau.

Before you know it someone's carried heavy bags up to the rooms, and such a pleasant little town, with so many curious corners, that after visiting the Victor Hugo Museum they decide to stay an extra night, giving them a full day to explore. The WC and shower are down the hall, but there are nice new terrycloth bathrobes in the closets, and seems like the old days, thirty years ago.

Up past the wall and to the Château. The Romans built a fort up there late during their Empire, and throughout the Dark Ages its ruins stood as a reminder of stern social order and security. By the time the early Middle Ages rolled around civic pride and perhaps an enhanced local economy had led to improvements, and by the 15th century the place had become quite palatial, as you see.

Then hard times set in again. Veinen had been the capital of its fiefdom, but times changed. By the middle of the 19th century the two main gates in the town walls had been pulled down and the château itself had lost its roofs and interior carpentry. Murmurs of deliberate pillaging, even, by one of the owners. In any case, it was again a ruin, this time not Roman but Romantic.

How, I don't yet know: fire, I should think. Some years ago, though, miraculously, the enthusiasm, technique, and above all money was found to restore the place. There were of course plenty of descriptions, sketches, and engravings to go on, and, I suppose, analogous buildings elsewhere (though not many of this caliber, I would bet). We spent an hour or so wandering the galleries, the huge rooms, the kitchen, the residence...

Thirty photographs or so: masonry, carpentry, fascinating photo-documentation, scale models of the building at three different epochs. No one wandering these halls and staircases: one can be entirely alone. Outside, men on rooftops, hanging slates on the battens. They work quickly but meticulously, the process defining a clear social order based on experience and skill. A boy, a helper, an artisan. Electric hoist of course. Hedgehog snuffling in the border.

This must go into the report: the boy carries slates to the helper, who hands them to the artisan, who corrects edges when necessary and hangs them on the pegs, presumably, not likely to use nails which inevitably rust and spoil the appearance. Rust through and fail causing slates to slip out, slide off, and break. Total failure. Shouldn't they be at the front? For that matter, where are they from?

She read in a travel article that Vianden is to be avoided on summer weekends, when the town is overrun with Dutch, Belgian, and German tourists. It can easily be believed. But in these early days after Ash Wednesday most of the hotels are closed and the town is given back to its three thousand residents. Curiously, many of these seem to be Portuguese. The economy is better here in Luxembourg.

International banking is the most significant part of the economy. Iron and steel remain important. Credit Sidney Thomas later. Tourism employs nearly an eighth of the working population; much hotel and restaurant activity related to business travel, either in private industry or service or connected with the European Union, whose Secretariat is in Kirchberg, Luxembourg-Ville, along with the Court of Justice, General Court, Court of Auditors, and the Investment Bank.

# 6. An easy arrow-shot

*1794: the French Republic liberates the castles in all the countryside around, and they liberate whatever they could find in and around them. 1798: the peasants don't like the idea of being forced into the French army and they revolt. Dasbourg was mentioned several times as a center of the uprising. The peasants lose.*

YOU COULD TELL SOMETHING was brewing, they kept throwing more dirt on top, digging it out from around the center, piling it up on top, stomping it down, driving donkeys round and round, everyone sweating and drinking and shouting and digging, the dirt piling up and spilling to the outside to keep the center clear, the floor kept getting lower.

The dirt gives up occasional spoils of its own: bones, shards of crockery, spearheads, rusty bits of iron... Now and then a scrap of cloth or leather, and you can only wonder how long such things can last underground. I'd have to ask my brother, who knows about such things, he says. I've slipped a few of these things under my shift, toward the end.

Onno is inspired: Let's drive the donkeys round the other
way! Never been done, comes the immediate objection,
from nearly the entire crew, not just the boss. But, he says,
it will even the packing, because the soil keeps slowly packing backward. He sees the earth's sinews, he says, not
straight up and down as we want, or neatly across as we
find digging, but slanting backward from the hooves.

Four men roofing one last part of the Château in beautifully fish-scaled overlapping curves, cutting each rectangular
tile with a mason's hammer against an anvil spiked anew
into the wood substrate as each course advanced. You'd
think the material must surely be synthetic to be so even,
but when I asked the crew flunky what it was, *C'est ardoise,
monsieur.* I knew that was slate, but then asked *synthethique?
Ah non, monsieur, c'est naturelle.*

Is it from here, then? *Ah non, monsieur, il vient d'espagne.* I
looked at him a little more closely: *Como Usted, creo. Ah si,
Señor,* he responded, smiling. Spanish slate, Spanish skill.
Portuguese inn (Auber would be pleased). European com-
munity at work. Not so different, I'm sure, from Roman
times.

We'd walked up to the château following an itinerary outside the town walls, laid up four feet thick and quite high of
local flags of shale, I think. Towers are placed every thirty
feet or so, an easy arrow-shot apart, close enough that no
sentry-walk was needed for further protection. The towers
are curious: often four or five stories high, they're open toward the town side: no infiltrators would have hidden in
them!

Even the donkeys shake their sweaty heads. Round and
round, head down to dirt, flies about the ears and eyes, the

smell of dirt and the sound of men. Shouts and that steady noise they call singing. One side works harder than the other: but What! One sunup we pull the other way! Same dirt, men, noise, smell; different pain... and always at sundown a little further from the paddock...

A boy runs in, shouting: The French have arrived at Veinen! He saw them from a hilltop, marching up past Rodeshausen church to the bridge and across it, tanned and healthy they look, not many bandaged, carrying only small knapsacks and their arms, with the fascinating flag and a drummer at the lead. There must be a supply train behind; he didn't wait to see.

All I can say is, *bacalhau* is clearly one of the Hundred Plates. It all depends on the cod, and the potatoes and onions, and of course the olive oil; a little garlic and parsley doesn't hurt; and the black olives of course; and I could swear I tasted thyme, and she thought she found a trace of red pepper...

Yes, it's a shame the main gates were pulled down a century and more ago, but it's a greater wonder that the walls themselves are nearly intact. They anchor a medieval taste that the entire town seems to maintain, with its lack of permanent signage, of sidewalks, asphalt, visible wires... perhaps they shoot movies here...

## 7. Other countries abroad

*1811: Napoleon I gives the castle and its goods, whatever is left, to marshal Nicolas Charles Oudinot, Duke of Reggio. Reggio is pretty far away, near Naples, a little inconvenient; so the Duke sold it on 13 April 1813 at public auction, provided that it be demolished within a year.*

THE AMERICAN GIRL opens a letter: her exchange sister continues to anguish over romance. The boys in Reggio are not like the Napolitani, they are just as thoughtless and condescending, but less certain of themselves. The *reggio* itself, the Versailles of Italy (or at least Calabria), its vast lawns, allées, watercourses, baroque statuary. Now there is something to be proud of, of which to be proud. Her window overlooked a small quiet service courtyard. She unpacked and rested up a bit, then went out exploring. This quarter wasn't really the center: Luxembourg is placed on a hilltop surrounded by an extraordinarily deep gorge, the valley of the Petrusse, which joins the complicated oxbows of the river Alzette to carve an astonishing natural defense nearly encircling the city. Again, "burg" here means fortress — "Luxem-" (or Lützel-) derives from a Germanic word meaning "little" — and the fortress on this plateau was considered...

She'd played Ophelia in her school production of *Hamlet*, and could never think of the word "country" without embarrassment. Was Calabria really a country, not merely a province, as papà had insisted, unless he was really joking, it was so hard to tell. How could lands be bought and sold and given away, given away with brides. Think of it, the strongest fortress in Europe after Gibraltar, the Brittanica says, and an hour's drive away a castle was auctioned off and torn down. Romantic, it says further: The situation is romantic, steep cliffs overhanging the winding river, and the principal portion of the town with the palace and public buildings covering a central plateau. But we are not on that plateau, we are on the railroad station side of the city; and when we walked out for a café we were disappointed to find nothing but typical fast-food places.

It is hard to write a letter to a sister who's not really your sister. A dozen or so Swedes were waiting for a guide, who turned out to be Swedish himself; and realizing that they'd all be better off touring in Swedish, we fell in with a charming woman in her thirties whose English was perfect and whose enthusiasm for her city was contagious. She would be our private guide. She took us to the Cathedral, talking animatedly about the history, the language, the architecture of the city, and walked us about most of the central plateau. A small cloud drifted overhead and I inevitably though of Mrs. Dalloway, we read too many novels papà always said, do you remember, but that can hardly be possible. Our friend here is Swedish by birth, she's lived here at least twenty years. Her father was Czech. Mobility is in the blood.

## 8. Curious and interesting

ON HIS WAY, says his letter, for this corner of Portugal in Luxembourg! With *bacalhau* in his suitcase, hope it's well wrapped, and his cap and shoes, though he'll find no *toros* here. And his hammer, let's hope, for there are no proper hammers either. Strange, such an up-to-date country, lacking proper tools. And bulls.

Day's end. You think you can go no longer, you can and do continue, you come to the stop. Smelling it long before seeing it, blinkered as you are and worn out. Freed from the traces, led to the stalls. Oats, sweet oats, and cool water. The men and their voices, incomprehensible. Stones underfoot, of course, will there ever again be grass.

Luxembourg-Ville, the last changing-post, so often heard about from other travelers, the changing-posts by the river below the famous fortress. Smell of horse, hay, suddenly broken by cheap perfume: can one put that effect on stage? He had enjoyed his stay in Veinen, but thought he'd given it

all the attention it needed at the moment, and in any case
time to move on.

Then there's the question of tomorrow's party, the entire
purpose of this detour. Who will be there, what will they be
wearing. Will I understand anything anyone says? What
kind of food will there be, and how to eat it? This could be
anyone thinking such thoughts, prey to such anxiety. Years
ago, surprised at the delicious things in the delicatessen
windows, paté de foie gras, caviare. Now we can afford it.

An iron ring had been set into the stone that formed the left
side of the door-frame: to tie your horse to, at one time, no
doubt. The walls were stucco, probably over brick. How
many bricks are there in this country, in the world, and who
makes them all. The stucco: sand and cement. The sand
and cement.: more stone, eroded or pulverized. Even the
glass: more sand. It's all made of stone, time, fire.

The bridge over the Our, stone of course, just outside the
window, and across the row of houses next to the road from
Dasbourg, where the fire burned last month, early in the
morning, the shouts and alarms, in my nightshirt I com-
manded them *calmez-vous!* and got them into line, the buckets came almost of their own volition to be passed hand to
hand from the river but two houses were lost and most of a
third... poor villagers...

It is a small nation, no doubt about it, but still it is a nation,
with good-sized provincial towns as well as the smaller villages. Ettelbruck is itself a city, after the bleak emptiness of
Dasbourg-pont, the quiet streets of Veinen. The bus put us
down at the train station, but there was plenty of time to
spend exploring. We walked into the center, pedestrianized
like so many European cities these days, scattered with cafés

and shops, and crowds, it seemed, bookshops, telephones, dogs, children.

Three nights at the Hotel Bristol, Rue de Strasbourg. The hotel is cheap and plain, the rooms small but comfortable, at the back of the hotel and so protected from street noise. Plenty of frugal guests, some lounging about aimlessly, others purposeful; young people with their telephones, older people with their little dogs or shopping bags or briefcases. The porter turned the baggage over to the bellboy; the bellboy sweated it up the stairs to the rooms. Careful with that chest! Put it there by the window; good light. All my papers.

A stone stele bearing a carved relief: olive branches encircling a vertical sword, a stylized American eagle perched atop, all set in a little park at the foot of a low hill planted in birches, and looking out across the railroad tracks toward the fields and ridges that had cost so dear so many years ago. All these pointless wars. It all seemed intensely curious and interesting: the American tank; the colossal bronze statue of General Patton. The museum closed, of course, closed; we turned back to the station and waited for our train into the city.

Look: a porter trucking a small traveling chest and a curious Oriental box, varnished wood, brass fittings. Luxury and refinement — *luxe, volupté*. The Luxembourg-Ville train station as we'd remembered it, with its fine stained-glass representation of the city on its hilltop, the viaduct leading to Clausen over the deep gorge; a splendid sun rising behind it. Stepping out onto the Place de Gare we were struck with the crowds, noise, buildings: Ettelbruck had been surprising enough, after days in open country and villages; this was nearly a shock. We are indeed in a city. It feels like Paris. Hotels, cafés!

A Portuguese immigrant, almost certainly, with a cheap dented cardboard suitcase, the corners reinforced with canvas beginning to give out. And look: a ten-liter jug. he's set down on the quay. Glancing down at it momentarily with a look of amused distaste a well fed Frenchman in a fine suit a little the worse for wear, fur collar, braided trim, carrying only a small polished leather valise, following the porter ahead of him. Clearly a Frenchman in spite of the wide-brimmed Italian slouch hat, the braid at its rim echoing the braided edge of his lapels. These guys are much too fancy. Too much prosperity?

## 9. War with Germany

OCTOBER 1859: A short, chunky guy in yellow boots, wearing an odd sweater, pink on its right side, blue-grey on its left, with an olive-drab left shoulder, a flap sailing off behind. And headless: no head to be seen at all. This could be an optical illusion: perhaps he's thrown his head way back, in a fit of some kind, asthmatic, epileptic, death-throes. Or perhaps simply an ecstasy, in the excitement of the festivities — the first train is about to leave the new railroad station in the country, with Prince Henry aboard, bound for Hesperange.

Listen: the little guy does have a head after all: for he sings:

> *Kommt hier aus Frankräich, Belgie, Preisen,*
> *Mir wellen iech ons Hémecht weisen,*
> *Frot dir no alle Säiten hin,*
> *Mir welle bleiwe wat mir sin.*

Don't read Lëtzebuergesch? It's easy enough to translate, it's doggerel, not poetry…

*Come here from Belgium, Prussia, France,*
*Just give our fatherland a glance,*
*Ask anybody, near or far:*
*We want to stay just as we are.*

And before he's got to the third line others have joined in, smiling at him in his odd colors, his open, dull, pleasant face...

Hesper! Well! Hardly an hour's walk from the cathedral, and they build a railroad! And the embarrassing thing is, there is no locomotive, no way to get a locomotive here, the rails simply go from Luxembourg into the forest, and there they stop, they haven't yet got the money or more likely the willpower to continue the rails into the Lorraine where the locomotives are. So sad Prince Henry sits in his coach and tries not to think about the poor gelding pulling his coach through the forest, tossing his head bitterly at the irony of it all.

One day perhaps the French, the Belgians, the Germans will arrive by proper rail, puffing locomotives blowing steam at the boys alongside the tracks. Why not? They've already taken most of our land; why not steam into what they've left for us, the rock, the fortress, this disgusting new railroad station, built hastily of wood because the Prussians won't let us take the time to build it properly of stone, and to tell the truth they're probably afraid we'd use it as a second fort, opposed to our fine old stone one they've taken over, and still control...

We sing in Letzeburgesch, they cannot stop that. We've sung in Letzeburgesch as long as any of us remember; we have been here thousands of years, according to that trans-

lator guy in the café; they've dug up bones and pots and
that sort of thing all over our country,

*(excuse yourself, he says sullenly, having bumped into an old man
    effortfully pedaling his ancient tricycle-wheelchair contraption)*

and then there were those skulls up in Engis, my brother
has seen those caves because of all the walking he did between Luik and Brugge, or said he did. I leave these ques-
tions to the "experts," who have time to sit and think and
talk about such things.

Let my brother go walking with his sack on his shoulder; I
have to hope the mines will open again and let me earn an
honest living. I take a beer at the sticky table in the bar,
there are crumpled pieces of paper everywhere, colorful
scraps, paper flags, I don't really care about most of it, I'm
not ashamed that I can't read, I work my days and save a
little money, I have a roof to sleep under and owe no one
nothing, and I am proud to be Letzisch and to hell with the
rest.

The beer is brewed right here, it never sees a bottle. Leave
the bottles to the French. It is almost thirty years since the
great betrayal when half our country was lost to the new
Belgium, but to hell with them too. Mud, mud and herring
and fried potatoes. Let them speak French, that incomprehensible language. They tried to teach it to me, and even to
read it and write it, a waste of time, it makes no sense to
me. I speak my mother's tongue, as she spoke hers. I don't
want to change, now or ever.

The land, the corn, the potatoes. His own land, don't think
otherwise! Father worked his own land! Bad as they were,
the French gave us the land, took it from kings and gave it

to us — though they took away our fatherland, gave it to the netherlanders. Brother has been there, all the way to Zutphen, good country for mud he says, dour cow people with no eye for forests, no mines but what they've stolen from Limburg, since they lost all the rest to Belgium... greedy bastards, Belgium, now they're taking all they can from black Africa...

The train, such as it is, is pulled away from the station, prince Henry riding off into the future. In eight years it will arrive, another aspect of it at least; Luxembourg will finally be granted its own independence, after William threatens to sell it to France, which would precipitate war with Germany, and no one wants that. What a restless time. No one will guess how much worse will come, beer in bottles, telephones on every side, locomotives quaint history like the American tank, and vast plantations of white crosses, dark granite stones. Lest they forget again.

## 10. Causes and culprits

KIDS WHO ARE TWENTY or thirty years younger than we have a totally different experience of life, manner of living.

How does any generation make decisions? Do they think about the legacy of destruction and debt left by their elders? How do they understand the economy? I think — from conversations I've had — that they may not understand very well. Social media encourage polarizing rhetoric, amplified by cynical politicians and the press and pundits, who corrupt their ability to discuss, absorb, process information. He said it here in his big, booming debate about it, or at least it may be that.

There's a lot of intellectual confusion about the causes and culprits institutionally of terms their elders can understand or abide.

The mess that we are in, I say! The language and the thinking that have evolved have had an impact on the way young people think! All this talk that society needs to change, and so on! A misconception of the role that business plays. We shareholders risk capital. Banks exchange capital. This is what keeps an economy going. Today, he went on, I was told the root cause of everything we're experiencing is a failure of holistic thinking. Oh!

Then that one of the fundamental assumptions after the financial crisis — a world of increasingly complex, fragmented, and ubiquitous information.

The Luxembourg state, as it was determined by William II, was that it would be officially bilingual, in French and German. And yet about the country people spoke Lëtzebuergesch — "Luxembourgish" — among themselves, as they still do. Lëtzebuergesch was not recognized until the 1980s, as I understand it, when suddenly linguists took an interest in it, declared it endangered, and began promoting its retention and even expansion. Declared a third official language, and began finally to be taught in the schools.

A problem immediately arose: it had never been a written language, and orthographical rules had to be invented for it.

As I've mentioned, I've run into people both here in Luxembourg and back in Belgium who spoke only their local language, Belgian Flemish, or German, or Lëtzebuergesch. They've been older people and country people, for the most part, who perhaps never did learn French or German as well as they might have, and who have lost it through years of neglect. They seem to me to be speaking Lëtzebuergesch. I think in this time of war they retreat into it.

I've always thought of language-speaking as a fairly simple affair : some people are monolingual, like most Brits and Yanks.

Others are functionally bi- or multilingual, like me, and most of the Dutch. I see now it's not that simple. Languages are intrinsically complex, they're mediations of divergent individual and social demands, they're always in flux, they're always a compromise between intent and the possible. How often these last days I've wound up saying not what I wanted to say but what I could say, or thought I could. Like the Yank drinking beer, not knowing the word for wine.

Try to understand! Listen to your elders! Learn from history! Make the future better! Don't just listen; think, consider, project!

Onno recalls his uncle, gone west first, to Flanders, then somehow across occupied territory, always safer than contested areas, as the priest had told him. Skagen, Dokkum, Stribo, Lisbon, Tarifa. The hateful memory of the fagne, no soil, no stones, only ooze, if you turned up something in the dark that felt at all hard it would be bones, buttons, or broken metal. Soggy tobacco, and the matches useless from the wet. Steal food from farmhouses, there's always something there.

## 11. Speaking and thinking

THERE ARE MONOLINGUISTS and there are polylinguists, and there are what you might call localinguists, who are monolinguists who speak only a small local language, enough to converse with the neighbors about matters of local importance, but at considerable disadvantage when it comes to communicating with other nations, or cultures, or eras.

If we chart the use of language in three dimensions, the X and Y coordinates are simple enough : language follows human social geography. In the land between Meuse and Rhine, Germanic (and Gothic) sounds prevailed in the east, French (and Romance) in the west. But traveling south from Zuid-Limbourg, the Dutch corner east of Maastricht, our lips and tongues have moved from Dutch to French and back more than once, because of the third dimension of language, which is time, as many of these territories have been moved politically from one sovereignty to another. For a long time Luxembourg was ruled by Spain.

And as lands move back and forth politically and, more re-
luctantly, linguistically, so do many of us. Individually. I
once asked a man who was born in a small mountain town
in northwest Italy, near Torino, whether his parents, who
settled in Canada in 1914 or so, spoke English or Italian at
home when he was a child, and he seemed surprised: Italian! Why, I didn't learn Italian until I went to school! We
spoke what we spoke[1]. Speaking and thinking seem so
closely connected that argument continues whether they are
mutually necessary. I think not, but then I think instrumen-
tal music is a form of speech, recording nonverbal thoughts
of its composers.

And that woman at her ironing table, a monolinguist speaking only forgotten Flemish from the flat country in western
Belgium, and unable to understand the harsh gutturals of
her neighbor, a localinguist who for whatever reason, probably the Depression and the war, had never gone to school,
or perhaps had simply forgotten everything the school had
managed to drive into her thick local head.

The deliberate national decision to recognize and encourage Lëtzebuergesch — the decision to require it in public
education — was the recognition, finally, that the Luxembourgish desire, stated in the nation's motto, "We wish to
remain as we are," is a national social value worth respect.
You could say the country had grown up. Until a generation ago Luxembourg was one of the poorest nations in Europe; now it is one of the richest in the world, its per capita
income surpassing that of the United States, surpassed only
by a few oil-rich emirates on the Persian Gulf. To remain

---

[1] Most speakers of that particular form of Italian Piemontese think of it
as a dialect; I've recently come to suspect that in fact it is a language,
Languedocien, fairly widely spoken across southern France from the
Pyrenees east to his valley in Piemonte. (Translator's note.)

as one was, in the face of so sudden a change, seems impossible and misguided, if perhaps understandable.   But try
explaining that to two old women up in Rodershausen.

But then remember the Council of Vienna, and the Treaty
of Versailles, and the one of Maastricht, and you realize
these cataclysmic nation-changing events are in fact fairly
regular, hardly a normal human lifetime doesn't see a couple of them.   And in fact as Daniel Arbess points out the
fact that we see smartphones in use everywhere we go is the
sure indication of another social cataclysm, and a linguistic
and economic one therefor, in which the three dimensions
of social interaction converge and collapse, you saw it in
Cairo for all the good it did, in Hong Kong ditto, in Occu-
py demonstrations in the United States ditto, and the good
grand duke goes on sitting in his sumptuous railway car-
riage, drawn by a draft-horse who's seen better times or at
any rate occupations you might call more practical.   Fifty-
one years since the last local armistice, true enough, but
that's an anomaly, wars and revolutions had come along a
hell of a lot more frequently in the years following the
French Revolution.   But then, before then, the boring generations of serfdom and plague… always one damn thing
after another…

## 12. We broke away

*AFTER THE WARS of liberation Dasbourg fell to Prussia. At this time, the Our was set as a natural border and Dasbourg a border town. Because of the steep terrain and poor soil the villagers could barely feed themselves by farming: so most worked as craftsmen, masons, laborers, or woodcutters. Thanks to the flourishing commercial life, the population grew constantly, and the village was usually full of artisans — though the village also owned a brewery.*

COMPLETE JUMBLING of local and national, class-based and subcultural-based strands, often thought fairly separate and identifiable — erroneously, it's evident. Class is significant. Indispensable, even, perhaps, to a stable society. Even in the age of archery, such moments made changes faster than their natures could have become evident: how much more urgent is such comprehension now. Lacking such comprehension one can only shake one's head, as did the old lady I was attempting to converse with in Rodeshausen the other day, and agree *das welt ist kaput.* I can't help thinking that she lacks language to investigate and consider that world; it has largely eroded away. On the other

hand, she seemed cheerful, happy with her lot, content to
remain as she is.

But the party had been a tremendous success, in the way
typical of these northern European fêtes, with skits and po-
ems and singing and dancing, a deejay, little kids, and a
sumptuous spread.   Much went on in Swedish, but there
was a fair amount of English too, and French of course, a
little German.   Cathérine herself is quite a linguist.   We
know her because she lived with us for a few weeks while
strengthening her English, over thirty years ago.   Her languages helped her professionally; she works for a Swedish
bank and assists at the Swedish consulate.   The next morning we took the bus out to Kirchberg where she put on a
fine brunch for some of the guests who'd lingered, say thirty
of us.

Then we broke away, to hear a Mozart concert in the
Cathedral, where l'Orchestre de Chambre de Luxembourg
played the little g minor Symphony no. 25 and then, with
combined choruses from the Luxembourg and Metz cathe-
drals, a fine, moving performance of the Requiem.   I was
impressed with the music, and the setting and its acoustics
— we sat close — were superb.   Luxembourg-ville continues to impress me; I can see why Cathérine has been content to make it her home.   It's easy to get out of town into
any of a number of attractive neighboring countries, but it
has plenty to offer of its own.   The central city is small, on
its two hilltops; it's easy to walk from one end to the other,
passing attractive parks and places, bars and cafés, shops
and restaurants.   We first visited the city forty years ago,
when we were delighted to find a delicatessen whose patés
and such were as good as the charcuterie we'd otherwise
found only in France.   (We were even more delighted, I remember, with the skies: one evening after a thunderstorm a

glorious sunset was finally signed, just before night really set in, with a magnificent double rainbow.) Since then the city has greatly developed, especially in the Kirchberg region. A few years ago we visited the new music theater, whose acoustics and stage facilities impressed me tremendously. But I'm glad we heard this Mozart Requiem in the cathedral; the setting was splendid. I am sorry to leave Luxembourg.

The use of languages for legal and administrative purposes is regulated by a law promulgated in 1984, including these provisions:

> Article 1: The national language of the Luxembourgers is Luxembourgish.
>
> Article 2: The laws are in French.
>
> Article 3: The language of the government: Luxembourgish, German and French can be used.
>
> Article 4: Administrative questions: If a citizen asks a question in Luxembourgish, German or French, the administration must reply, as far as possible, in the language in which the question was asked.

In many other multilingual countries, such as Belgium, Switzerland or Canada, the distribution of the languages is geographic, but in Luxembourg, perhaps too small for geographical distinctions, it is functional — that is, the choice of language depends on the situation.

Look at the language of the law! Clear, concise; *clair, concise.* And notice: "The national language of the *Luxembourgers*", not "of Luxembourg". A nation, that is, a country, does not speak; it is the citizens who speak. And note the good-natured practicality of the law: "the administration must reply, *as far as possible...*" Truly Law and Administra-

tion have advanced beyond the seigneurial system; the pos-
sibility of administrative inability is not only imagined, but
considered, even included within law... by statute, "as far as
possible." Had some clerk — for surely it's ultimately the
clerks who refine these Articles, however they may have
been drafted by their elected superiors — had some clerk
recalled a chance conversation with a country cousin, perhaps in Rodeshausen? *Tollerday donsk*, he may as well have
windered. Because of the steep terrain and poor soil the
localingual villagers could barely feed themselves by farming, and so most worked as craftsmen, masons, laborers, or
woodcutters; their children as clerks and clerics, capitalists,
schoolteachers.

# 13. Unhappy eyes

VIANDEN, ALWAYS VIANDEN, the old city up the steep valley, river to castle, and the new one across the river, the gentle Our. I wrote my best book here, that terrible year, comfortable in my little house on the bridge, but sadly regretting Paris, flat Paris with her broad avenues and beautifully dressed women. Adèle among them, of course; she had such a fine eye for dress. A fine eye and hand, in fact: it was not simply a matter of the dressmaker, any intelligent woman can cultivate an eye for dressmakers; it was her hand as well; her hand itself well disposed to dressmaking, which she'd learned as a child. I suppose. All I can do is suppose, now, poor Adèle, gone like so many others. Ford, Jacobsen, Spears, Caraciola, Baraglia. How we enjoyed our Sunday walks, on warm sunny days, around the Place, then perhaps to the canal, to the Hôpital, always remarking on the marvelous entrance of that mansion on our way, and then Adèle always responding porte de service, monsieur, on our way home; always the two remarks, unvarying, on

our otherwise silent but quite enjoyed afternoon walk, when
the weather was good.  Not every time.

All I could do there, Vianden I mean, in that quiet little
house, all I could do was write.  There was nothing else to
do, nothing but write, or remember.  There was no society
apart from the villagers, no books but those I'd brought
with me.  There was walking to be done, of course; the
woods thereabout offer plenty of footpaths, dating back
hundreds of years they say, perhaps thousands — no question Caesar himself had been along this placid river — but
the weather was not always conducive to a pleasant walk.
And then I had other things on my mind.

Thirty thousand dead, more or less, in the bloody streets, in
that single bloody week.  Flaubert said you had to put it in
perspective, from a Chinese point of view, these things
happened regularly throughout human history, it's just that
we're so young comparatively that it seems so horrifying
and disgusting.  How old are we then?  Vercingetorix, Joan,
1789?  Every birth a bloody one, rarely both mother and
infant surviving long.    But the children, the newborn!
Jeanne!  Your soft unhappy eyes!  On my way home from
the Tour St. Jacques I bought a doll that opens and shuts
her eyes…

> If you go on like this, always this pale,
> in our tired stifling air,
> if I see you come into my bleak shade,
> me old, you just a child…
>
> If I see things growing confused these days
> I, on my knees
> gazing at you, and wishing my death soon
> and yours far off,

*If your hands, fair, transparent, and frail,*
*in your cradle*
*Trembling — you seem expecting to grow wings*
*like a small bird;*

*If you don't seem to take root on our earth*
*for very long,*
*your soft unhappy eyes wandering about*
*this mystery of ours*

*If I don't see you gay and pink and strong;*
*if you dream, sad;*
*if you don't close the door behind you, Jeanne,*
*when you come in;*

*If I don't see you as a fine woman*
*walking, in good health,*
*laughing...and if you seem a little soul*
*unwilling to stay here,*

*I'll think that in this world where shrouds sometimes*
*can serve as swaddling clothes...*
*you've simply come to go, to be the angel*
*guiding me away...*

Mawkish, perhaps. And yet it's how I feel these days, old, bereft, outliving children and grandchildren. Alexandrines[2] and half-alexandrines. And, why not, it's not just about sick children. It's all the innocent ideals, the hope for true fraternity, a world at peace, ordered for the benefit of all, cab driver, prince, clerk, king, foot-soldier — for foot-soldiers there must be — road-builders, dyers, poets. Poor Charles covered with blood in the cab. It is impossible to get any work done these days; perhaps I'm simply too old, have

---

[2] in the original. Pentameter here. (Translator's note.)

outlived myself, my writing self, as well as my son.   Why
should we continue to create, well past the years we procre-
ate?  My Veinen, you've seen better days, no doubt about it,
yet you're content, rain or sun you lie along your Our,
climb (no longer busily) toward the castle, provide your ag-
ing people with shelter, modest fare, sufficient interest.

The old man doesn't have that much longer to live.  Being
old and having done much that doesn't bother him.   No
doubt the next thirty years will be eventful but they will un-
fold perfectly well without a great Romantic poet.   The
pleasures and the days of the decade to come are already
being celebrated by less imposing writers and painters.
Dancing at the Galette, now that's better than moodily out-
lining Mme. Recamier or Marat dead in his tub and a lot
less agonizing than bare-breasted Marianne with her flag-
pole not to mention those starving wretches on their im-
plausible raft.

It's all lies, all of it, all literature, all journalism, all commercial announcements god knows, all the reports and dis-
patches among soldiers, explorers, priests, schoolteachers,
petty officials, cabinet ministers, gardeners sent out to trim
the topiaries, cooks at their stoves and sinks, carpenters and
shoemakers at their benches, women at their sewing-frames,
their hospital beds, their cigar-rolling, label-gluing, glove-
making, lovemaking.   Every verse you write returns to in-
dict.  The new Chateaubriand with clay feet, a whited sep-
ulcher of pious clichés and fleeting fame.  How many will
turn out for my funeral?  Of them, how many will give my
words a second thought?

In the corner room windows on the north look out over the
street and the bridge and the Our, those on the west over
the street leading up the hill toward the castle.   The Por-

tuguese Inn is just across the bridge. Hugo sits in white plaster, his elbow bent, his fingertips thoughtfully resting on his temple, the books behind him now, eternal white plaster, easily dissolved away.

## 14. Water between your hands

THE WATER BACK there, it flows from the ground like milk from a young mother's breast, soft and sweet through the faintly rotten grass and mosses. Last winter's snow, I suppose, or the snows of centuries, slowly piled up on the plateau, melting drops at a time from the weight, soaking into the grasses of hundreds of summers. There is a solace in this, reassurance of the constant renewal, perhaps constant isn't quite the word, the recurring renewal in each cycle of seasons, or years, or generations, or centuries. Snow falls; water accumulates; spring releases; summers sublimate; winters then return.

A perfectly straight road cuts across the fagne: the old Roman road. God only knows why they built it so, come so many months' march from Rome, soldiers, mules, slaves, women, traders, spies, musicians. It can't have been so different from Alexander's day, when thousands of people marched across Asia to the river, then back, investing, gambling, quarreling, suing, breeding, teaching, feigning, harvesting, cobbling, stealing, conniving, drinking, dreading, praying, singing, praising, pleading, bribing, promising, betraying, hoping, cursing, growing sick, tired, defeated, and dying. Alexander of course marched through rich resourceful nations: these Romans simply slogged on through this endless mud.

It's only a day's walk on a pleasant day, no near or distant fire to startle the horse, dismay the women, require explanation from the scouts. In these bad times it's a different matter entirely. Suppose it's October, or March, outside of snow season, raining all day and all week, the snows are melted and the rains fallen, nothing but cold dismal water everywhere. What bread there is is soggy. There is no difference between the water on the ground, the water in the air, the water between your hands as you pull the soggy bread from the pack, perhaps wring it out, jam it between your soggy lips into your wet mouth, tongue and tooth it until somehow you choke it down into your waterlogged belly where it lies wet inert and complaining until it descends inevitably growing, swelling, blocking every process. Like the wet powder refusing to ignite.

On a warm sunny day in late spring or summer or early fall the walk is simple, the sun gives you your direction not that there are many turns to take, the ground is dry enough to walk, you're wet toward noon and worse after noon with sweat but a rest can dry you out. If there's no fire you're in good shape, you forget the problems, the frights, the broken limbs and rotten packs you saw a week before, or was it a month, in good times time itself stretches its limbs lazily, daylight fills the day, murders night.

In such weather, on such days and even weeks, the fagne itself is broader, its boundaries indistinct, the forest no more than an annoying memory. The sweet scent of grasses restores the sense of smell, finally overcoming, replacing, eras-

ing the stench of war, war and death, death and decompo-
sition. Arms and legs, unbearable faces, rotten rags and the
occasional shoe, all shoving their way behind his eyes, however he might sing or drink. And the likelihood of more to
come. Can clear away, given just the right morning, clear
and bright, perhaps a cuckoo calling from the trees behind,
a breeze on my back, toward noon, under the sun, the hum
of bees, the scent of flowers. There were times when the
ground almost dried out. It is not the same ground here.
The road may be two thousand years old; legionnaires may
have trooped here from the Tiber through Segusium and
past Daysberhc; all along the way the ground was different
and the same, the same to the planners with their charts,
intent on distances and weather, but different to those who
dealt with it *in fact*, clenching it with calloused fingers to as-
sess its water and fertility, digging it with bone or stone or
bronze or a sharpened stick or even their calloused fingers;
to those who dug it with spades, tossed it into baskets, carried it to the rising wall ringing the pit, as Aage has ex-
plained, building up the wall around the central floor, shap-
ing civilization.

A man with a wheelbarrow. A man with a wheelbarrow is
nothing extraordinary; he alternates throughout the last
century with various powered machines, front-loaders,
back-hoes, ditchers, steam shovels, trenchers. In the beginning was the blade, the basket, the barrow. In the bogs,
spades, cutting the turf; boys and men and women too to
carry the blocks of turf, hope for sun to dry them. Stacked
for fuel they serve as curtain walls. Chains sometimes of
men and boys handing them along, like Victor Hugo's fire-
buckets. Dripping with water from the Ours, or slime from
the great fen.

Activities in peace and war, famine and prosperity, plague and better times. They know they have no control over such things; the superstitious and the ignorant grasp at whatever they can — comets, eclipses, blood moons, sudden infestations of insects, unusual weather, the utterly foreign aerial geometry of flocks of starlings, bats, inexplicably monstrous births. In between, for the long stretches of seasons, the routines: thaw, mud, breezes, drying, flowers, fruit, vintage, chestnuts, snow, darkness, ice. Birth, life, death. The square box bed by the old hearth. Rarely anything new; the earthen ring walls still visible, like Aage's Danevirk. Men with blades and baskets raising walls, walls across England, across Slesvig, around their holes. You've got to put it somewhere. Some of us stuck to our land, digging it out, piling it up, or scraping their roads through it for the Romans, swords and shields, mules and horse, busy imperious ignorance.

What makes all this work? In theory, some kind of organization, discipline, force. In fact, though, I bet it's mostly routine — they make their parades as a habit, a routine, Rome to Augusta and back, just as we scratch our carrot-patches, from one end to the other and back. And as our women and children scratch the soil with their digging-sticks, dribbling the fine dark seed, so their little men at traveling desks scratch at their leaves of wood and leather, tallying, for these people have a mania for counting, with more numbers than you could ever imagine.

You have to wonder about these soldiers, striding along in formation, their generals or whatever they are on horse-back, servants and slaves and women straggling along behind, carefully watched of course of what it really takes to make the whole thing stick together, and the little men with their scratching-sticks tallying the men and mules and barrows and days.  What a grand and stupid business it must be, getting it all together, walking it for weeks and months through the countrysides, taking whatever women they want, the best fruit and wine, then slogging on, the whole damned parade of them.  First with their strange southern gods, then claiming they are in fact gods themselves, finally taking up the desert god, and calling us fools and rustics for carrying on with what was good enough for our grandparents and theirs too, they tell us, wanting to remain as we are.

## 15.  The tax, the tribute

*In the time of the Romans the Vianden valley was covered with vine-yards, but at the present day its chief source of wealth is derived from the rearing of pigs.*

IN A THOUSAND words you would not be able to describe it, any of it.  The tedious ordinariness of the daily life, the sudden joys at marriages and successful childbirths, the sor-rows at deaths and disappearances, the discomforts of hunger and fatigue, the injustice of crime and war, the reg-ularity of disease.  We slept in boxes, three or four hours at a time, waking to stoke the fire or take a pee.  We ate pigs and beets.  We minded our crops, aware we'd keep only what we could hide.  There was game in the forest but it was dangerous to hunt.  In summer the days were long and the work endless; in winter the nights were long but there were songs and stories.  Thousand-word stories, no doubt, the old people could go on for hours, the kids were en-tranced.  Thirty years would make a life for many of us, but we mostly left children behind to live another thirty.  I don't see how you could ask for any more.  War and pestilence

will be what the future will know fixed as it will be on its
own violent agenda but we lack the means to know or discuss history.  The priests and our grandparents, those that
we may have, tell us the old stories, the legions and the
Gauls ; Christ and the twelve disciples ; the fox and the
crow ; babies lost to the fens.

Our first time, driving north along the river against its cur-
rent, not far from Wasserbillig where the oleanders grew so
improbably, and across the broad expanse of the calm
Moselle a freight train, tiny in the distance, behind its
steam-locomotive puffing coal-smoke into the clear air, lazily and methodically made its course parallel to ours, there
we saw the grapevines climbing the steep steep slope, so
steep cables had been run between the rows of vines, I suppose that carts might be attached, or perhaps the crews
worked tethered, like linemen on their frighteningly tall
stanchions.  If stanchions is the word.

The American tourist and his wife stood in the rain, a sudden blinding downpour, trying to shelter under a linden
tree.  Nearby, pulled off the road onto a shoulder barely big
enough to protect it from blinded drivers, a Daf stood
parked in the rain, a small camping trailer behind it.   A
woman opens its door, gesticulates to invite the rain-soaked
couple into the camper.  They accept a pot of tea, ashamed
of the pools of water collecting at their feet, and the language waltz begins: Do you speak English? No. *Sprechen sie
Deutsch? Nein. Parlez-vous francais? Non. Sprekt U nederlands?
Ah, nederlands, jazeker… maar…* and all the words drain away,
they too, into the sodden carpet at their feet, and the tea
proceeds, silently, Irrelevant thoughts come to mind.

Did I not dance with you in Brabant once?  And oh these
children's voices, singing in the chapel… I shoulder my

wool or my loss of wool and look out diligently... ideas of order, or we die... roll on sweet river 'til I end my song... We saw no pigs, nor evidence of pigs, except at table, where sausage and ham and schnitzel never fail to appear. He looked at her, then back at the menu. He's not thinking of food, she is telling herself, in her quiet unshared mind, he's thinking of wine, whether red or white, with pork there's no question, that's the Mosel, just order the vin de table. Clear thick glass bowls; green stems; white wines.

*I'd crossed the Nahe in the usual mists, surprised at the new walls they've raised around Vincum...*

Approaching a close never fails to impose its certain regret. Roll on sweet Moselle, from sweet Lorraine. *amnis odorifero iuga uitea consite Baccho*, o river, Bacchus's fragrant vineyard ridges, until the song must end. Until the Romans came the vines grew as they would, innocent of order or ideas of order. Order and industry, standing between childhood and old age. Tend these vines and trees, the old man said, that's what you're here for. Genesis itself a tract urging ideas of order, not inherent order of earth, water, seed, sunlight, time, growth, decline, but ideas of order: property, rights, storage, work, schedule, increase, loss. They demand the tax, the tribute, we're left to figure out how to raise it.

This Spanish road along the broad Moselle, the narrower, fresher Our, up into the forest and the fagne, water every step of the way, running down the road beneath the feet, falling into the hair despite the trees. Not to mention the mud, sticky embrace of earth and water, odorous, treacherous, alluring. Death by warm drowning, into that sweet earth. Northbound and out of it! Yet Hans, or Jean, or Juan, gone toward the south and Spain and freedom to return again to stand and fight and turn the bastards back, devious, victorious Jean, patient and unknown, flow on, sweet waters, 'til I end my song...

Distracted, recalling the surprising new walls around the city to the north, he didn't notice his mule's slackened pace until they were motionless in the dusty road. Something made him remember a scene from many years before: he was on a playing field; a leather ball was being tossed and kicked back and forth between two teams of boys; as one of the captains (there were too many captains) he was at the line adding his own ideas to a desultory discussion: what were the rules; what constituted a score; how was the ball permitted to be moved; even which boys were on which team; how many constitute a team; can anyone play at any position. Glancing toward the side of the field he saw his grandparents, they looked his own age, returned to life, wearing ancient togas.

# Translator's notes

*Veinen*: Coqt's version of the place-name usually known as Vianden; *Veianen* in Luxembourgish.

page 6, *we had a tiptop…*: the italicized passage is in English in the original.

page 8, *except for a few*: thus, tantalizingly, in the typescript.

page 9, *Douwe en Egberts*: the Dutch coffee company.

_____, *down the steep road look*: ends without full stop in the original.

page 36, *memory of the fagne*: the Haute Fagne, south of Spa, a large plateau composed of peat, storing snowmelt from the Belgian winters, the source of Spa mineral waters.

page 40, *Daniel Arbess*: quoted in "Magic Mountain," an article describing the scene at the Davos gathering of the World Economic Forum, written by Nick Paumgarten and published in the March 5, 2012 of *The New Yorker*. This citation is of course my own contribution to the original text, which has an inexplicable lacuna here.

page 46, *If you go on like this, always this pale…*: Victor Hugo, "*À l'enfant malade pendant le siège*," from his collection

*L'année Terrible*, written during his sojourn in Veinen. My translation.

page 57, *I'd crossed the Nahe*: Transieram celerem nebuloso flumine Navam, addita miratus veteri nova moenia Vinco… (Ausonius: *Liber X Mosella*)

*finis*

www.ingramcontent.com/pod-product-compliance
Lightning Source LLC
Chambersburg PA
CBHW050905120626
46554CB00003B/1023